KT-154-792

SAMURAI SHOWDOWN

BY JOHN SAZAKLIS

ORCHARD

MEET THE TEAM:

Bumblebee

Sideswipe

WITHDRAWN FROM
BROMLEY LIBRARIES

TRANSFORMERS
ROBOTS IN DISGUISE

Author! - S SAZAKEIS

Bromley Libraries

30128 80285 013 4

ORCHARD BOOKS
Carmelite House
50 Victoria Embankment
London EC4Y 0DZ

First published as DRIFT'S SAMURAI SHOWDOWN in 2015 in the
United States by Little, Brown and Company.

This edition published by Orchard Books in 2017

HASBRO and its logo, TRANSFORMERS, TRANSFORMERS
ROBOTS IN DISGUISE, the logo and all related characters are
trademarks of Hasbro and are used with permission.

© 2017 Hasbro. All rights reserved.

A CIP catalogue record for this book is available
from the British Library.

ISBN 978 1 40834 492 7

1 3 5 7 9 10 8 6 4 2

Printed and bound by CPI Group (UK) Ltd, Croydon, CR0 4YY

Orchard Books
An imprint of Hachette Children's Group
Part of The Watts Publishing Group Limited
An Hachette UK Company
www.hachette.co.uk

The paper and board used in this book are made from wood from
responsible sources.

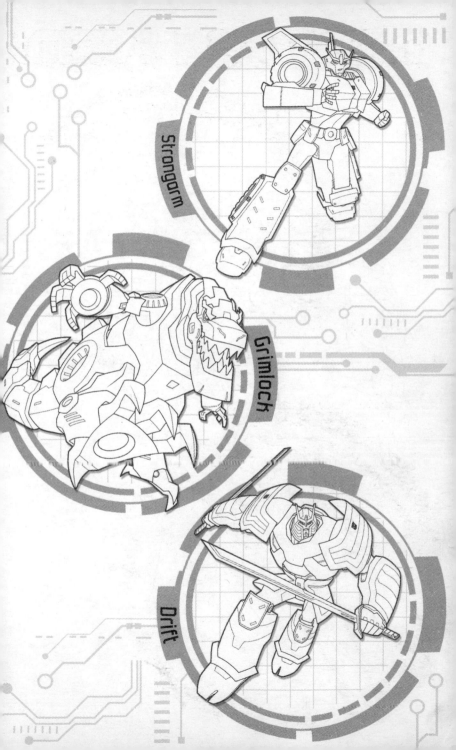

Strongarm

Grimlock

Drift

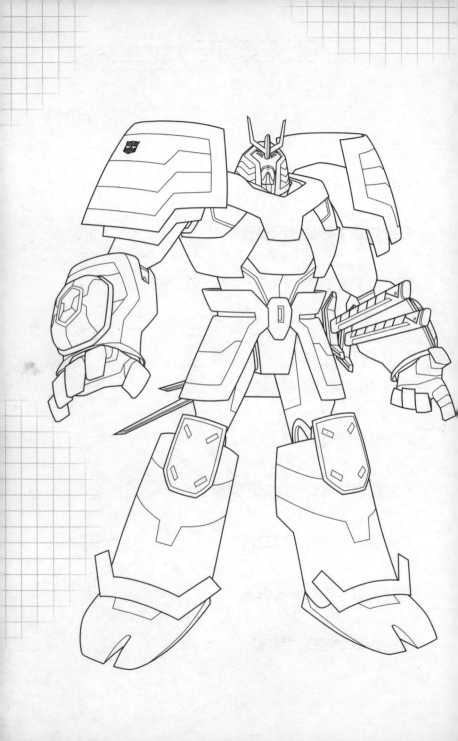

CONTENTS

FLICK TO SCROLL

STATUS REPORT: A prison ship from the planet Cybertron has crashed on Earth, and deadly robot criminals – the Decepticons – have escaped.

It's up to a team of Autobots to find them and get them back into stasis. Lieutenant Bumblebee, rebellious Sideswipe and police trainee Strongarm have taken the Groundbridge from Cybertron to Earth to track them down.

Along with bounty hunter, Drift, reformed Decepticon, Grimlock, and the malfunctioning pilot of the ship, Fixit, as well as the two humans who own the scrapyard where the ship crashed, Russell Clay and his dad, Denny, the robots in disguise must find the Decepticons, before they destroy the entire world ...

CHAPTER ONE

"DECEPTICON ATTACK!" BUMBLEBEE shouted at his team. "The scrapyard has been breached!" He zoomed through their makeshift Earth headquarters with his high-beam lights flashing and his horn blaring. "All bots to their stations! This is NOT a drill!"

Strongarm was the first Autobot to respond to Bee's alerts, switching straight from sleep mode to her robot form. The eager cadet was always at the ready.

"I'll protect the humans, sir!" she said, sprinting toward the vintage diner that Denny and Russell Clay called home. "I can see Sideswipe isn't up to the task!"

"Hey, this bot's always got his motor revving," replied Sideswipe, flexing his gears and shaking out his sprockets. "It just so happens to be the middle of a night cycle, and I was getting my beauty recharge."

Flashy young Sideswipe flipped through the air and landed back to back against strait-laced Strongarm.

Suddenly, the ground beneath them started to rumble at the approach of pounding footsteps. The two Autobots drew their weapons.

"AWW YEAH, LET ME AT 'EM!" Grimlock roared, stomping his way towards the scrapyard's front gate. The massive Dinobot was always itching to turn some Decepticons into scrap metal!

Bumblebee screeched to a halt in

Grimlock's path, blocking his stampede. "That's not the plan, Grim. Follow our breach protocol!"

Bumblebee spun his wheels while the Dinobot complied and turned around. Grimlock joined his team-mates at the diner, grumbling all the way.

Denny Clay stumbled out into the scrapyard he owned and operated, rubbing the sleep from his eyes and tying the belt on his vintage flamingo-pattern robe a little tighter.

"What's all this racket? It's after midnight, you know," Denny pleaded, stifling a yawn. "Humans actually need to sleep, remember?"

Bumblebee quickly pulled up next to the diner and shifted into his bot mode.

With his lights still shining, the Autobot leader peered into the darkness of the scrapyard. There were no Decepticons in sight. There was also no sign of Drift, the mysterious former bounty hunter who had recently joined up with them.

"Where's Drift?" Bumblebee asked. "This drill needs everyone's full co-operation to work."

Strongarm and Sideswipe exchanged looks as they slowly realised the 'Decepticon attack' might not be as real as they had thought. They returned their weapons to their holsters.

"Um, sir, did you say 'drill'?" Strongarm asked tentatively.

If any bot understood the need for being prepared, it was Strongarm, but that didn't mean she appreciated being left in the dark by her commanding officer.

Russell Clay, Denny's twelve-year-old son, stepped out from behind a row of antique washing machines. He clicked a stopwatch in his hand.

"Three minutes and forty-five seconds, Bee," Russell said. "Two minutes longer than your goal time."

"Scrap, that's no good. And Drift didn't even show up! I don't know about that bot ..." Bumblebee sighed. "In the case of a Decepticon attack on the scrapyard during typical Earth rest hours, we should all be able to meet at Central Diner Defence Point Delta in under two minutes."

Grimlock was still ready to rumble. He looked around and slowly realised what was going on.

"You mean I don't get to demolish any Decepticons tonight?"

"No, Grim," Bumblebee explained. "This was meant to be a 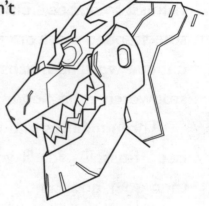 training exercise, but not all your team-mates thought it was worth their time."

As the rest of the Autobots went back to bed, Drift calmly joined the gathering, followed by his two faithful mini-cons, Jetstorm and Slipstream.

"Nice of you to FINALLY show up,"

Sideswipe mumbled to Drift as he
went past.

"It is wise of you to try to train your
team, Bumblebee," Drift replied dryly.

"It is clear that they struggle with basic functions."

Drift's insult upset Strongarm, who prided herself on her combat readiness. She was about to argue, but Bumblebee raised a hand to stop her.

"I, however, do not need training. I have survived on my own for many cycles," Drift continued.

Jetstorm coughed as if to remind Drift that he had been alone except for his mini-cons. Slipstream stepped on Jetstorm's foot and quieted him. Drift was a stern master.

"I know you're used to working alone, Drift," Bumblebee said. "And I'm happy to have you as part of our team. But I won't stand for you insulti—"

BEEP! BEEP!

An alarm screeched over the speaker system installed on the diner's exterior.

"Decepticon attack! Please retort ... resort ... report to the command centre at once!" The jumble of words was the telltale malfunction of Fixit, the Autobots' mini-con helper.

Denny Clay covered his ears with his hands.

"Is this another drill, Bee?" Denny yelled over the siren. "If so, it's way past Rusty's bedtime – and mine!"

"If this is a drill, it's not one I planned!" Bumblebee yelled back. "We'd better join Fixit and find out what's going on!"

CHAPTER TWO

ONCE EVERYONE HAD GATHERED IN the command centre, Fixit tapped furiously at his console to pull up a large hologram of the Decepticon that his systems had discovered. The villainous bot had mask-like markings over his eyes and a large tail circled by rings of alternating black and brown metal.

"Aw yeah, I DO get to smash up a Decepticon!" Grimlock said, pounding his fists together.

"He looks like a raccoon!" Russell said.

"What's a 'raccoon'?" Grimlock gulped nervously. "That's not anything like a ... kitten, is it?"

The huge Dinobot looked scared. He wasn't very good at hiding his bizarre fear of Earth felines.

"Actually, they're not closely related," Russell said, easing Grimlock's mind slightly. "But they do look and act a little similar, I guess."

Grimlock suppressed a startled yelp.

"My sensors picked up a Decepticon moving through the side streets of Crown City," Fixit explained. "It appears that he is trying to stay hidden from humans, but who knows how long that will last!"

"All right, bots, we need to apprehend this Decepticon before he's spotted," Bee said, stepping up to lead his team.

"Oh, he's not spotted, Bee," Sideswipe remarked, pointing at the image.

"He's stripy, see?"

Bumblebee narrowed his optics.

"What?" Sideswipe shrugged. "I may only be half-charged, but my funny bolt is always at one hundred percent!"

Ignoring the hotshot Autobot, Bumblebee continued on with the task at hand.

"Grim, you'll have to stay behind. We'll be in the middle of the city, and you don't have a vehicle mode," he said.

The Dinobot tried to hide his relief.

"Fixit, what can you tell us about this criminal before we *put wheels down and go to town*?" Bumblebee asked.

Sideswipe groaned over Bee's newest attempt at a catchphrase.

"Decepticon identification: Forager.

Mercenary, bounty hunter and general bad guy," Fixit said as he punched at the console, processing data. "Arrested alongside other Decepticons calling themselves the Ronin."

Drift scoffed. "This Decepticon is not worth my time. I will provide you with my students, Jetstorm and Slipstream, to assist in my absence."

Before Bumblebee could protest, Drift turned and walked out of the room.

"I guess someone never learned about teamwork," Sideswipe whispered loudly.

"OK, team, we don't have time for this. We've got to put wheels down and—"

"Bee!" the rest of the room shouted, cutting off their leader's new rallying cry.

"Fine, let's just go and capture this Decepticon," Bumblebee said, leaping into vehicle mode and leading his team out of the scrapyard.

Slipstream and Jetstorm jumped onto Sideswipe's trailer and Strongarm brought up the rear. Grimlock and Fixit stayed behind as Denny and Russell Clay shuffled back to bed.

The Autobots cut through the forest, crossed the bridge and arrived in Crown City in no time. Using Fixit's co-ordinates, they quickly spotted Forager in a dark alley behind a garage.

The Decepticon was sifting through spare motor parts.

Bumblebee quietly directed Sideswipe to take to the rooftops. The younger bot zoomed out of view, switched back to bot mode and leaped into the air with Slipstream and Jetstorm close behind.

Strongarm, in her police car mode, pulled around to block Forager's exit.

Once the whole team was in place, Bee honked his horn – **BEEP BEEP** – startling the Decepticon!

"Guess I gotta bust up some natives!" Forager growled, tearing an old tyre in two with his bare paws. "Let's dance!"

"Heads up!" Sideswipe yelled, drawing his swords and dropping down on the Decepticon from above.

Drift's two loyal mini-cons followed close behind.

Sideswipe slashed and sliced his blades at Forager.

SWISH!
CLANG!

The Decepticon deflected the blows with his claws as showers of sparks lit up the night sky.

Slipstream and Jetstorm lunged at Forager's legs.

The Decepticon hopped from one foot to the other, trying to kick the mini-cons off.

"Looks like we *are* dancing after all!" said Jetstorm.

While Forager attempted to hold off his three ninja-like assailants, Strongarm and

Bumblebee revved their engines and charged at the Decepticon.

In a flash, the two Autobots crunched Forager between their bumpers!

SMASH!

The cowardly convict was knocked high into the air.

"Good work, team," Bumblebee said.

The Autobots loaded Forager's unconscious frame onto the trailer, tied him down and covered him with a tarp.

Bumblebee radioed Fixit and asked the mini-con to prepare a stasis pod.

A short victory lap later, the bots arrived back at the scrapyard with their defeated target.

"My, that was fast!" Fixit exclaimed, greeting the bots near the stasis pods. "Not much fight in this one?"

"This is just what happens when you work together, Fixit," Bumblebee said, scanning the scrapyard for Drift. "Too bad not everyone on this team seems to have got the message."

As if on cue, Drift rounded the corner.

Slipstream and Jetstorm bowed to their master.

"I am glad the mission went well," Drift said. "I trust my students were of sufficient help?"

Slipstream bowed and pulled back the tarp to reveal a still unconscious Forager. Drift gave a barely perceptible nod of approval.

Once the mini-con had replaced the cover, Forager opened his optics. The raccoon-like bot had only been pretending! He flexed his dextrous paws and two lockpicks popped out from the tips of his claws. With a swift twist of his wrist, Forager freed himself and made a break for it, tossing the tarp at Drift and the mini-cons to distract them!

"So long, losers—"

WHAM!

Forager ran right into Grimlock.

"Looks like I got to demolish a Decepticon after all!" Grim said, holding Forager down with one massive foot.

Bumblebee helped Grim load the struggling captive into the designated stasis pod.

"Let go of me! I have my rights, you know!" Forager yelled, straining against Grimlock's powerful grip. "You can't lock me up just 'cause I'm a convicted criminal!"

Before the pod's cover slid shut, Forager got a good look at the other bots. His optics locked on Drift.

"Hey! I know you!" Forager hollered, pointing at Drift through the pod window.

"You're the guy that did that Ronin job on the moon of Athena! You gotta get me outta here, pal!"

Before Forager could say anything else, Fixit finished the stasis sequence and put the dangerous Decepticon on ice.

Bumblebee quietly mouthed Forager's words to himself, processing what had been said. He turned toward Drift.

"What did he mean by 'pal'?"

Drift tensed his shoulders. The mysterious samurai rested one hand on the hilt of his sword.

"My past is my own, Bumblebee. Do not assume you have any right to know about it."

Strongarm and Sideswipe moved closer to Bumblebee's side.

"If you're going to work alongside my team, I think I have every right."

Jetstorm and Slipstream cast worried glances at their master, who refused to meet their optics.

"If that is your stance, perhaps it is time I leave this team, Bumblebee." Drift quickly shifted into his vehicle mode and sped out of the scrapyard.

As the dust settled, everyone exchanged grave looks.

Everyone except for Grimlock. "What just happened?" the dinobot asked.

CHAPTER THREE

DENNY CLAY'S ALARM CLOCK went off at seven o'clock the next morning. Crawling out of bed, Denny's first thought was that the Autobots' Energon couldn't be better than a good cup of coffee!

The Clays enjoyed having Bee and the others around, but it could make for a lot of sleepless nights, something that exhausted Denny a bit more than it did his son, Russell.

As Denny shuffled outside he stumbled upon a full-on Autobot interrogation, like something out of one of his favourite vintage cops versus gangsters films.

Slipstream and Jetstorm were sitting side by side on an overturned refrigerator. Bumblebee leaned over the tiny bots, scowling, while Grimlock, Strongarm and Sideswipe stood menacingly behind him.

"Youse better fess up or it's no more Mr Nice-Bot!" Bumblebee said in a bizarre accent.

"Whoa, guys, what's going on here?" Denny asked, sprinting toward them as fast as his retro bunny slippers would carry him. "And what's with that corny gangster act, Bee?"

"Sometimes you leave the TV on at night and that stuff starts to sink in," Bumblebee replied. "We tried asking nicely, but these two won't say a word."

"Why are you questioning your own team?" Denny asked, surprised at Bumblebee's behaviour. "And where's Drift? I don't think he'd like you talking to his students like this."

"That's exactly the problem, sir," Strongarm piped up. "Our newest Decepticon prisoner seemed to recognise Drift as a former ally, but Drift sped away before we could get any explanation out of him. Now we're questioning his mini-cons to try to discover if Drift is actually a spy – a Decepticon double agent!"

Just then, Bumblebee glanced at Slipstream and Jetstorm and saw how frightened the mini-cons looked. He gave a sigh. Being a leader wasn't easy.

Even the legendary Optimus Prime
occasionally made the wrong call.

"I'm sorry. We might have ...
overreacted," Bumblebee
said. "We're happy to
have Drift and the two
of you on the team,
and it's admirable that
you want to protect him,
but we do really need to know what's
going on."

Slipstream and Jetstorm looked at each
other, their optics widening and
narrowing in wordless conversation.
Jetstorm opened his mouth to speak, but
Slipstream glared at him to stay quiet.

Soon, Russell Clay wandered outside,
sleepy-eyed and confused.

"What's going on out here, Bee?" Russell asked.

When Bee had filled Russell in on the mini-cons' strict silence, Russell stepped forward to take charge.

"Why don't you let me have a shot with them?" Russell asked, cracking his knuckles. Slipstream and Jetstorm would have been intimidated, but it's hard to be scared of an Earth boy in cartoon-print pyjamas. "Give me a few minutes and I'll have them singing like nightingales."

"I don't need them to sing; I just need them to talk," Bumblebee said, prompting an eye roll from Russell.

"I know I can do it," Russell said with confidence. "But you'd better give us some space. Except for you, Sideswipe.

You should stay."

Everyone else reluctantly headed to the opposite end of the scrapyard. Denny shot Russell a look of concern before he went, but Russell gave his dad a thumbs-up. Once the others were out of sight, Russell climbed on to Sideswipe's shoulders.

"OK, boys, it's time to play rough," he said, looming over the mini-cons. "Tag, you're it!"

Russell leaned down and slapped Jetstorm on the shoulder, then shouted at Sideswipe to run. After a moment's confusion, Sideswipe grinned and ran off down one of the winding corridors between the junk and old trash of the scrapyard.

Jetstorm and Slipstream shared a puzzled glance before Jetstorm cracked a sly grin, too, and ran off after Sideswipe. With a drawn-out sigh, Slipstream followed.

"Tag, you're it!" Jetstorm shrieked, knocking Sideswipe on the knee.

"Not for long!" Sideswipe replied, leaping backward to bop an unamused Slipstream on the head. "Tag! Your turn!"

Slipstream grumbled, but he couldn't deny wanting to play, too. He ran after his fellow mini-con and tagged him, keeping the game in motion until Russell was a sweaty mess and the three bots were running on fumes.

They all met back by the diner and plopped down near the overturned fridge.

"So, how does that count as interrogation, Russell Clay?" Jetstorm asked, stretching out his joints.

"It doesn't. I figured you get enough of that just by being Drift's students," Russell replied. "He's really tough on you two."

Slipstream and Jetstorm looked at each other and slowly nodded.

"Master Drift is tough on us, but it's for our own good," Slipstream said, defending their master. "And whatever he's doing now, whatever reason he has for leaving, must be a good one."

"So you don't know why that Decepticon acted like he knew Drift?" Russell asked.

"Master Drift shares lessons with us,

not his life story," Slipstream replied.

Jetstorm coughed and nudged Slipstream in the side. Slipstream tried to act like he hadn't noticed, but Jetstorm did it again – and again. Finally, Slipstream came out with it.

"OK, fine!" Slipstream whispered angrily. "Master Drift did tell us one thing that is probably important ..."

Russell and Sideswipe leaned in to hear Slipstream.

"Before Master Drift was Master Drift," explained Slipstream in a whisper, "he went by another name: Deadlock.

And under that name, Master Drift wasn't the honourable Autobot hero you know today – he was a Decepticon!"

CHAPTER FOUR

"DRIFT USED TO BE A DECEPTICON? ARE YOU SERIOUS?" BUMBLEBEE shouted, leaping out from behind a pile of old bicycles. "You mean I let a traitor into our ranks?"

Strongarm climbed out from her own hiding spot under a stack of vintage carousel horses.

"You couldn't have known, sir!" she said. "Decepticons are deceptive – why, it's right there in the name! Although, there is protocol in place for background checks. If you had read handbook entry eight hundred and sixteen, subsection eighty-seven, you'd know that ..."

"Not helpful, Strongarm!" Russell said. "And were you guys spying on us? Didn't you trust us?"

"Yeah, didn't you trust them, Bee?" Grimlock asked, peering down from the roof of a nearby retired school bus. Russell shot him an accusing look. "Hey, don't look at me. I just come up here to catch some sun once in a while." The Dinobot lay back down on his perch and stretched out, excusing himself from the conversation.

Bumblebee stood up to address Russell and the mini-cons.

"I do trust you, Russell, and I appreciate the honesty, Slipstream and Jetstorm," he said. "But this is very serious. If Drift was communicating with

Forager, he might also have been communicating with Steeljaw or other, even worse Decepticons. He could have been getting close to us to feed them information about how to attack Earth."

"Master Drift would never betray his word!" Slipstream shouted. "He is a bot of honour. He would never betray … us."

Slipstream hung his head in disappointment. Jetstorm moved to comfort his brother-in-arms, but Slipstream pulled away.

Sideswipe mulled over everything he had heard from Slipstream and Bumblebee, along with the scene he had witnessed last night. The usually hasty bot tried to recall exactly what Forager had said to Drift before the pod closed.

"Hey, Bee, I just thought of something," Sideswipe said. "Forager said he recognised Drift from a moon or something, but it wasn't an instant thing, right? He had to think about it first."

Slipstream and Jetstorm looked up at Sideswipe hopefully.

"So maybe Drift does have, you know, a past – just like Grim – but it's all behind him now, and he's just ashamed to admit it? We've all done things we aren't proud of."

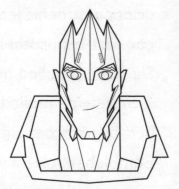

Bumblebee considered this thoughtfully.

Grimlock leaned over the roof of the bus to nod encouragingly.

"Well, sir, Sideswipe may be right," Strongarm said, "but we have to consider the possibility that Drift is no longer allied with Forager and is afraid of compromising plans with other Decepticons."

Slipstream and Jetstorm both groaned in frustration.

"I'm sorry, sir, but we can't afford to take chances," Strongarm added. "We've already witnessed infighting among the Decepticons, so we need to be prepared for any outcome."

"I'm afraid Strongarm is right," Bumblebee said, addressing the mini-cons. "It might be hard to hear, but we have to brace ourselves for the worst until we can find Drift and get his side of this.

And it doesn't make me optimistic that he sped off when we tried to discuss it."

The Autobots and Russell slowly trudged back toward the diner, their minds swirling with thoughts of betrayal and mistrust.

Suddenly, Fixit's voice crackled over the speaker system.

"This is not a drill! Multiple Decepticon signals located!"

The Autobots all rushed to the command centre, where Fixit pulled up a holographic map. Two red beacons flashed in the quarry a few miles from the scrapyard.

"Fixit, can you pull up information on these new Decepticons so we know who we're facing?" Bee asked.

Fixit's digits click-clacked across the keyboard. He buzzed with confusion.

"I'm afraid not, Bee," Fixit replied. "It looks like these Decepticons have obscured their signals!"

"Can you look up another signal for us?" Strongarm asked. "Can you track Drift?"

The mini-con went back to typing away speedily. After a moment, he shouted, "Aha!"

"Our systems are too weak to pick up most general bot signals unless they're in the immediate area, but by rerouting the signal booster through the Energon relay—"

"Cut to the chase, please, Fixit," Bumblebee interrupted politely.

"Base … case … I mean, 'chase' indeed, Bee!" Fixit replied, pointing to the screen. "There's a signal that matches Drift's size and shape moving right toward the two Decepticons!"

Slipstream and Jetstorm gave each other worried looks – as did Bee and Strongarm, but for different reasons.

"We must find and assist Master Drift!" Jetstorm pleaded. "We don't know how powerful those Decepticons might be, and he's headed right for them!"

Bumblebee agreed with the mini-con. He ordered everyone to gather up and head out … except for Jetstorm and Slipstream.

"I need you two to stay behind and protect Russell, Denny and Fixit.

We'll go and help your master."
Bumblebee instructed.

The two smaller bots reluctantly
nodded as they accepted the Autobot
leader's commands.

Bumblebee changed into his shiny yellow vehicle mode and led Strongarm, Sideswipe and Grimlock out of the scrapyard gate, racing into the woods toward the three signals.

Once they were out of earshot of the others, Strongarm drove up close to Bumblebee and whispered to her commanding officer.

"Sir, you know there's a possibility that Drift is moving toward the Decepticons on purpose, right?" Strongarm said. She hesitated, not wanting to finish saying what she was thinking. "That he might be meeting up with his—"

"Don't say it, Strongarm," Bee interrupted. "I know what you're thinking. And I'm afraid your suspicion might be right. Drift isn't accidentally heading toward trouble – he's meeting up with his Decepticon allies to cause it!"

CHAPTER FIVE

AS BUMBLEBEE, STRONGARM, Sideswipe and Grimlock raced toward the Decepticon beacons, Russell did his best to keep Drift's anxious mini-cons occupied at the scrapyard.

"Tag, you're it!" Russell shouted, bopping Jetstorm on the shoulder and running off. But the mini-con didn't move to follow.

"I am not 'it', Russell Clay," Jetstorm replied morosely. "Unless 'it' means 'depressed'."

Russell frowned. He turned to his dad for help.

"Hey, you guys!" Denny said in his

characteristically cheery voice. "I just got a shipment of retro video-game cartridges, and I need help blowing on them to see which ones still work. Think you guys are fit for duty?"

Jetstorm and Slipstream were too honour-bound to resist a call to help. They both stood at once and bowed to Denny.

"We will assist you in your task, Denny Clay," they said in unison.

"Yeah, that sounds great!" Fixit added. "Maybe while we do that, I can tell you all about how I once subdivided the power coupler to—"

"Sure thing, Fixit," Denny said, cutting him off. "Whatever floats your boat."

"Oh, Denny Clay," Fixit chuckled.

"This was on a transgalactic space shuttle, not a boat! Really, humans are so odd sometimes."

While the Clays kept the mini-cons occupied, the Autobots zoomed through the woods toward the flashing beacons. Bee screeched to a stop at the edge of the forest, where the trees cleared and the land sloped down into the quarry.

"OK, bots, this is where Fixit's tracker leads," Bumblebee whispered, changing into robot mode and peering down at the device in his hands. "That means Drift should be right ... there!"

Bumblebee pointed across the quarry, where Drift's sleek sports car form was kicking up a storm of dust. "But where are the Decepticons? The tracker shows that Drift is nearly on top of them."

"Maybe they're camouflaged!" suggested Strongarm.

"Maybe they're really small!" offered Sideswipe, looking on the floor around them.

"Maybe they're ghosts!" added Grimlock, prompting blank looks from his team-mates. "What? Rusty always makes me watch scary movies with him. You never know!"

Bumblebee quieted his team. As they watched, Drift rushed right past the Decepticon signals and ploughed into the forest on the other side of the quarry.

"There's something strange going on," Bumblebee said, leaping into vehicle mode once more. "Follow me!"

The Autobot leader steered down into the quarry, taking the same path Drift had just blazed. The dust was still settling when they arrived at the location of the beacons. Bumblebee, Strongarm and Sideswipe switched back into their bot modes.

"Great, so Fixit created another busted invention," Sideswipe said, looking around the seemingly empty quarry. "Can we get a move on and catch up with Drift?"

"Wait a minute, exhaust-for-brains," Strongarm said, crouching down. "What are these?" The law-bot held up a pair of small metal discs with blinking red lights on them. "They look like—"

"BOMBS!" Grimlock shouted. He snatched the discs out of Strongarm's hands and hurled them across the quarry. "EVERYONE, DOWN!" The Dinobot hit the ground with a thud and the other bots followed. After a minute with no explosion, Sideswipe raised his head.

"Uhh, guys, shouldn't we have blown up by now?" the young Autobot said, peering around.

"Be quiet, Sideswipe!" Strongarm hissed. "Explosive ordnance protocol clearly states that—"

"Hold that thought, cadet," Bumblebee said, springing up and running in the

direction of the discs. Bumblebee picked
one up, checked the tracker in his hand
and then hurled the disc back in the
direction of the other Autobots,
scattering them. "I knew it!"

Strongarm carefully peered out from
behind a boulder. "Knew what, sir?"

"These aren't bombs. They're fake
Decepticon signals," Bumblebee said,
picking up the remaining disc and crushing
it between his digits. "Someone left them
here to distract us and get us away from
the scrapyard." Bumblebee quickly dialled
Fixit on his communicator, but the quirky
little mini-con didn't pick up. "Forget Drift,
we need to get back now!"

Unknown to Team Bee, another set of bots was on their way towards the scrapyard. Just inside the tree-line surrounding the yard's outer fence, two escaped prisoners were conspiring and plotting.

They were the dangerous Decepticons known as Foxtrot and Stilts. Foxtrot was a cunning and sly rust-coloured bot, with a big round tail and pointed, alert audio sensors. Stilts was tall: long legs, long neck, long beak – with a gleaming white metallic sheen and a bright red feather-like crown on his head that glinted in the sun.

Both bots were safely under the cover of Stilts's electric wings – which hid them from anyone looking for their signal.

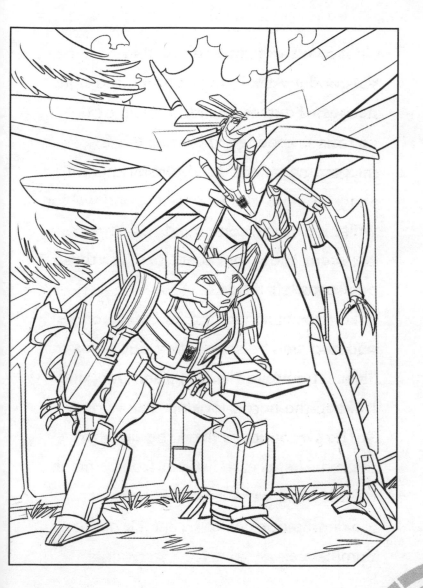

"It looks like those disgusting do-gooder Autobots just found my signal decoys," Foxtrot hissed, tapping at a console embedded in his tail. "The microcameras captured two of them. I'll program holo-cloaks of each, and we can waltz into their compound with ease. My scans show that there are just three mini-cons left inside."

Foxtrot punched in a few more codes and two small discs popped out of his tail. "Here, you take the big green one, and I'll keep the nerdy-looking yellow one."

The Decepticons fixed the discs to their chests, pressed the buttons, and, in a flash, they were covered in perfect looking holograms of Grimlock and Bumblebee!

"A Dinobot?" Stilts said, looking down at himself with a wicked laugh. "Guess I'll have to act extra dumb to match my new look."

Inside the diner, Fixit got a ping to say that the perimeter sensors had been tripped. He pulled up a visual of two bots walking toward the scrapyard's entrance, limping and looking wounded. To him, it looked like it was Grimlock and Bumblebee! Denny told Russell to stay put and asked Jetstorm to watch him.

Denny, Fixit and Slipstream sprinted out to attend to the disguised Decepticons at the front gate.

"Bee, are you OK?" Denny asked.

"What happened to Sideswipe and Strongarm?"

"And Master Drift!" Slipstream added.

The bot they believed to be Grimlock cracked an awful smile full of sharp teeth. He unhooked a capsule from his waist and tossed it at Slipstream and Denny.

WHOOSH!

It exploded into a giant net on impact, trapping the two of them tightly inside!

"Nothing … yet," Stilts sneered.

He dropped the hologram, revealing himself as a tall, bird-like Decepticon.

Fixit tried to zoom away, but the pretend Bumblebee snatched him up.

"Not so fast, scrap metal," Foxtrot said, dropping his hologram. He dangled the mini-con upside down.

"You're going to show us where you're keeping Forager. The Ronin may not follow any masters, but we take care of our own!"

CHAPTER SIX

"DID YOU HEAR SOMETHING?" Russell asked, nervously peering out of the diner windows. Jetstorm gently pulled the young human back.

"Let me take a look first, Russell Clay," Jetstorm said, steeling himself for action. "I am honour-bound to protect you under your master's orders."

Russell rolled his eyes. "He's not my master, Jetstorm. He's my dad!"

Jetstorm slipped silently through the diner door. He quickly froze in his tracks when he saw Stilts approaching with Denny and Slipstream strung over his shoulder in a net!

Jetstorm darted inside and pulled Russell into a back room. The front door creaked slightly as it closed.

"What was that?" Stilts asked, bending his long, crane-like neck toward the sound. "I thought there were only three mini-cons left on this base."

Denny twisted around in the net.

"I, uh, dropped my hubcap," he said.

Stilts peered over his shoulder at his captives.

"You're an odd-looking bot," the Decepticon observed. "A little ... soft to be a Cybertronian."

"Beep boop bop?" Denny replied.

He wiggled in the bag, doing his best impression of a robotic dance that had been popular in his youth.

Stilts glared and kept walking.

Once they had gone, Jetstorm emerged from the back room and peeked outside again.

"Your master and my brother-in-arms have been captured, Russell Clay!" Jetstorm whispered to Russell. "The ones we thought to be Bumblebee and Grimlock must have been Decepticons in disguise! We must escape! Climb onto my back and hold tight."

With Russell clinging to him, Jetstorm quietly slipped through the diner's back door and began hopping, ninja-like, from junk pile to junk pile, heading towards the exit.

On the way, they spotted Foxtrot carrying a struggling Fixit toward the stasis pod controls. Jetstorm and Russell wanted nothing more than to help their team-mates, but they knew they were no match for Decepticons on their own.

Once they were safely outside the scrapyard, the pair hunkered down in the woods.

"This isn't right, Jetstorm," Russell pleaded. "I have to go back and rescue my dad!"

"I understand, Russell Clay," Jetstorm responded. "But we need help. We need to find Master Drift! Er, and the other bots, of course."

Jetstorm attempted to contact Bumblebee on his wrist communicator, but he only heard static.

Without a message or a map, Russell

climbed onto Jetstorm's back once again and the two of them headed off in the same direction as their friends, hoping to meet them along the way.

Back inside the scrapyard, Stilts overturned an old shark-diving cage to form a makeshift prison for Denny and Slipstream.

"This should keep you out of my gears for now," the Decepticon remarked.

Foxtrot turned to Fixit and pointed a sharp claw at the mini-con. "Release the Ronin," he commanded.

But Fixit refused to unlock Forager's stasis pod.

"No pay … ray … way!" he said.

Furious, Foxtrot pulled out a blaster and aimed it at the captives.

"I'm feeling a little rusty and could use the target practice!" he sneered.

Fixit reluctantly complied, too nervous to protest again. After a few keystrokes, the door to Forager's stasis pod slipped open with a hiss and a pop.

"Ah, whatta nap!" Forager said, stretching and yawning. "I knew I could count on you fellas to spring me."

Forager, Foxtrot and Stilts exchanged an overly complicated handshake with lots of quick movements and jerky jabs.

"Ronin take care of their own, Forager," Foxtrot said, stuffing the no-longer-useful Fixit back into the prison with Slipstream and Denny.

"It's funny you guys mentioned that," Forager replied, popping a lockpick out of his finger and picking absentmindedly at his shiny metal teeth. "Right before I got pinched and stuffed in that cooler, I saw an old buddy palling around with

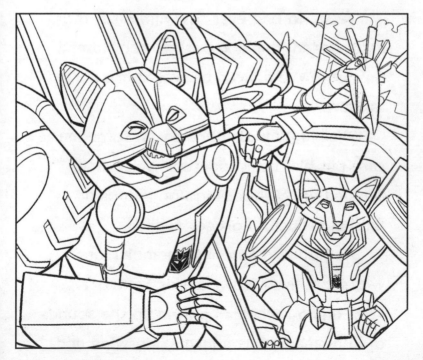

these Autobots. Remember Deadlock? He was that samurai-bot, really into honour and stuff."

Foxtrot and Stilts both looked stunned.

"I thought that bot got blasted on the moon of Athena," Foxtrot said.

"Yeah, no one ever saw him after that," Stilts added, thinking back to that fateful mission. "We figured he was spare parts for sure."

"Well, if he was spare parts, someone sure put him back together well – and slapped an Autobot logo on him as a finishing touch," Forager replied.

The Ronins' trip down memory lane was short-lived, however, as Foxtrot's keen audio receptors picked up the sounds of Bumblebee, Strongarm, Sideswipe and

Grimlock attempting to sneak back into the scrapyard.

"The Autobots have returned, brothers," Foxtrot informed his fellow mercenaries. His face twisted into a garish grin. "Shall we escape or take this place over as our new base on Earth?" Stilts and Forager let out wicked cackles.

"As if that was even a question!" Stilts exclaimed. "This'll make the perfect hideaway while we plunder and pillage as we please!"

"Sounds peachy, Foxtrot, but it's still three versus four, and I don't like them odds," Forager reminded him. "I ain't goin' back in that freezer."

"Don't worry, I have an old holo-cloak in my records that'll make this fight a lot more interesting …" Foxtrot replied.

The Decepticon punched a few codes into the display screen on his tail and two small discs popped out. He stuck one to his chest and pocketed the other. "I'll save this hologram disc as a surprise."

With the press of a button, Foxtrot donned a perfect hologram of Drift, or – as they knew him – Deadlock!

"How do I look?" he asked.

"Like a sight for sore optics," Forager replied.

Across the scrapyard, Bumblebee and the others walked nervously towards the diner with their blasters drawn.

As they turned a corner, they saw

Drift standing with his back to them.

"Drift!" Bumblebee whispered to their cryptic colleague, but Drift didn't move or respond.

The Autobot leader walked closer ... reaching out to put his hand on Drift's shoulder when – *WHOOSH!* – it went straight through!

"It's a hologram!" Bumblebee shouted to the others – a moment too late.

A second, solid Drift leaped out from behind a stack of cars and pinned Grimlock to the ground.

"This is an ambush!" the pretend Drift yelled.

Before the big Dinobot could pummel his opponent, he was shocked with an electrical charge.

ZZZARK!

Sideswipe and Strongarm hurried to help their fallen friend, but Stilts and Forager appeared and grabbed them by the wrists.

With a quick spin, the Ronin threw the two young cadets into each other, knocking them both out!

WHAM!

As the pretend Drift and his allies tied up Bumblebee's team-mates, the Autobot leader dashed behind a scrap pile and called for help.

"Mayday, mayday!" he yelled into his communicator's open channel. "Drift and his Decepticons have attacked the scrapyard. If anyone is left, send help!"

"Sorry, friend," the disguised Foxtrot

said, leaning over Bumblebee's hiding place with Forager and Stilts behind him. "Those nice big wings of Stilts's block signal transmissions. You just spent your last moments of freedom sending out static."

The villains laughed and quickly piled on Bumblebee, overpowering the struggling hero. Soon, Team Bee was dragged to the stasis pods. As quickly as they had been captured, the Autobots were locked away and the Ronin were left in charge of the scrapyard!

CHAPTER SEVEN

OUT IN THE WOODS, JETSTORM and Russell continued trudging along, hoping they would run into other Autobots. As they neared the quarry, Jetstorm picked up on a fragmented communication:

"Mayday, mayday ... Drift ... attacked ... scrapyard ... help!"

"Hey, that's Bumblebee's voice!" Russell said. "But that means Strongarm must have been right – Drift really is a traitor!"

Just as Russell put Jetstorm's worst fears into words, the two of them looked up to see Drift speeding towards them!

"Run!" Russell shouted at Jetstorm.

Jetstorm reluctantly complied, and the young boy hung on tight as the mini-con sprinted through the branches.

Drift's motor roared as he gained on them.

VROOOM!

Jetstorm bounced off trees left and right, cutting into a denser part of the forest. Together with Russell, he hid under a big, overturned tree trunk.

Suddenly, a large shadow passed overhead and landed in front of them.

It was Drift!

Russell and Jetstorm screamed.

"Why do you flee from your master?" Drift boomed, making Jetstorm shrink.

The mini-con might be easily

intimidated, but Russell was not. The human climbed off Jetstorm's back and confronted Drift.

"Because you betrayed us!" Russell shouted.

He beat his fists on the cold metal exterior of Drift's shin. "You and your *real* team kidnapped my dad! Now give him back!"

Drift was instantly taken aback. "My 'real team'?" he asked.

"The Decepticons!" Russell yelled. "The tall one with wings and a beak and the mean-looking orange one with the big tail."

Drift's normally calm exterior broke. He bent down and put one massive hand around Russell's back to comfort him.

"Russell Clay, I did not attack the others, but I think I know who did," Drift said to the distraught young human boy. "You must believe me if we are to rescue them."

Russell looked up into Drift's face, unsure of what to do, but Jetstorm slowly walked over and kneeled in front of Drift.

"I trust you, master," Jetstorm said, eyes averted.

Drift looked at him for a moment.

"Stand, student," he said. "I have not earned your trust. It is time that I came clean about my past. I had hoped to put it behind me, but I see now that my silence has put others at risk. Come with me and I will tell you all."

Drift shifted back into his sleek vehicle

mode and opened the door for Russell to get in. Jetstorm took his place on Drift's side.

Driving back to the scrapyard, Drift explained how he had come to know the other Ronin.

"Many cycles ago, Cybertron was a very different place," he began. "When the Decepticon movement first began, it wasn't clear how evil they were. They spoke about equality and political reform on Cybertron. It was easy to get swept up in all the talk, especially if you started life as a homeless bot stealing Energon just to survive. The skills I learned on the streets drew the attention of Megatron, the leader of the Decepticon movement."

Russell's jaw dropped at the mention of Megatron. He had been around the bots long enough to know that Megatron meant serious trouble.

"Megatron brought me in, giving me a purpose – and a new name: Deadlock," Drift continued. "I worked alongside the Decepticons for many cycles, watching the movement grow increasingly destructive and distanced from its original goals. I did many things I am ashamed of, and for which I can never atone. When I was nearly destroyed in battle, a group of peaceful bots called the Circle of Light repaired me and allowed me to live among them, trading unending conflict for honour and self-control."

Drift sighed, sifting back through painful memories.

"Eventually the war reached even the Circle of Light, and my peace was shattered. For countless cycles after that, I wandered aimlessly, a samurai without a master or a cause. Which is exactly what the Decepticons called the Ronin were looking for."

Drift rolled to a halt in the trees surrounding the scrapyard.

"What you must understand about the Ronin is that they answer to no one. Like me, they were Decepticons who grew disenchanted with Megatron's goals. There were many of them, and no single leader. They accepted me without questioning my past deeds. It was … comforting. But in time, I discovered that what they did, they did without honour."

"What did they do?" Russell asked nervously.

"They are bounty hunters, but they recognise no code of virtue. During my final job with them, a group of us followed a bounty to the moon of Athena, a distant planet with a large native population. The target retreated to a sealed bunker deep under the moon's surface. Rather than retreat, one of the Ronin, Foxtrot, suggested blowing the moon apart from space. The explosion would have been devastating to the inhabitants of the planet below."

Russell gasped.

"So what did you do?"

"The only thing I could," Drift replied. "When our ship neared bombing range, I set off a small explosion that scared everyone else into the ship's life pods. After they were clear, I triggered the rest of the explosives and then escaped myself. Our ship detonated in orbit. The Ronin were stranded in space until other members of the guild could rescue them, but I fled ... determined to follow my path alone, and with honour."

His tale done, Drift let Russell out and shifted back into robot mode.

Jetstorm again kneeled before his master.

"I trust you, master," Jetstorm said.

Drift bowed to him.

"I trust you, too, student," Drift responded.

Russell looked at Drift. "I trust you," he admitted.

"And I you, Russell Clay of Earth."
Drift replied, sounding relieved. "Now I
ask that you maintain that trust. It will
not be easy to defeat the Ronin that
have captured your – our – friends. We
will need to deceive them."

CHAPTER EIGHT

DRIFT, JETSTORM AND RUSSELL
approached the entrance of the
scrapyard. The bright afternoon sun had
set, giving the normally welcoming gate a
sinister vibe. A bot that appeared to be
Grimlock immediately greeted them.

"Hello, big bot, small bot and soft bot,"
pretend-Grimlock said in his dumbest
voice. "Me am your Dinobot friend! It am
safe to come inside."

"I do not think so, Stilts," Drift said, a
serious look on his face. "That is you
under there, is it not?"

The pretend Grimlock frowned and
dropped his holographic disguise.

"I thought Forager had brain rust when he told us he had seen you, Deadlock," Stilts replied. "But it must be you with a malfunction if you've allied yourself with these pathetic Autobots."

Without warning, Drift snatched an unsuspecting Russell in one hand and pinned Jetstorm to the ground with the other.

"You mean these two?" Drift asked.

"I was just tracking down the strays. The Decepticons have a sizeable standing bounty for these bots, and I mean to collect it."

"Is that so?" Stilts asked, not quite believing Drift's story. "Forager said you seemed pretty chummy with them when he got locked up."

"Do you know of an easier way to capture this many bots on your own?" Drift responded without missing a beat. "I was about to start picking them off when Forager blew my cover. Now let me in and we'll discuss how we are going to split the payday."

Stilts still looked unconvinced.

"A nanocycle ago I thought you were nothing but debris drifting through space in a galaxy far, far away," Stilts said. "You're going to have to talk to Foxtrot before I trust anything that comes out of your speech module."

"Oh, is Foxtrot your leader now?" Drift challenged.

"The Ronin have no leader," Stilts said through an angrily clenched beak. "We take care of our own."

The tall Decepticon reluctantly let Drift in with his struggling prisoners.

When they passed the makeshift holding cell, Drift roughly tossed Russell and Jetstorm inside. Russell just caught the slightest hint of a wink as the former bounty hunter left them locked up.

Inside the command centre, Foxtrot and Forager were flipping through the prison transport records, taking note of which other members of the Ronin were on board when the ship crashed on Earth. Foxtrot wasn't happy to see Drift.

"Shouldn't you be in stasis, traitor?" Foxtrot hissed, flexing his claws.

"Whoa, whoa, wait a minute, Foxtrot," Forager interrupted, stepping forward to stand in between Foxtrot and Drift. "I'm sure our old pal Deadlock – or should I say Drift – has a solid explanation for why he's here and how he's still in one piece."

"There is not much to say," Drift stated in his typically stoic fashion. "Our ship went down. I thought you blew up. You thought I blew up. I work alone now. End of explanation."

"You've worked alone until now, right, old buddy?" Forager said, chuckling.

He wrapped a thick arm around Drift's shoulders. "This is fate! We're getting the gang back together. With all them stasis pods and fancy equipment, we can sell the Autobots to the Decepticons and the Decepticons to the Autobots. We'll be rich!"

The cunning criminal cackled at his own idea.

"We'll be richer if we don't split the bounties with this back-stabber," Foxtrot growled.

"And how long will you waste learning about this equipment and this planet?" Drift asked. "These foolish bots taught me everything."

"Did they teach you how to use the trash compactor?" Stilts asked. "We were just brainstorming fun ways to deactivate the mini-cons. No bounty on those runts."

Drift's face remained calm and unreadable.

"No, but I do know the locations of all the Energon caches they've discovered," Drift said.

The Ronin's optics went wide.

"And we'll need more Energon to power the locators and track down the rest of the bounties," Drift added. "I've been itching for some action after holding back around these law-bots. Anybot who wants to join me is welcome to follow."

Stilts and Forager looked at each other and grinned. These rough-and-tumble Decepticons were always up for causing a mess. Foxtrot didn't hide his distrust of Drift, but he reluctantly joined in.

On the way out of the scrapyard, Forager stopped to taunt the prisoners.

"Enjoy the scenery while it lasts, you byte-sized bots," Forager said, rattling the makeshift cage containing Denny, Russell and the mini-cons. "When we come back, we're gonna have fun recycling you!"

Drift stood idly by while the Ronin harassed his former charges.

When Forager grew tired of the game, they all shifted into their vehicle forms and rolled out.

Forager turned into a Cybertronian
dirt buggy, Foxtrot became a sleek alien

sports car and Stilts took flight as an otherworldly jet plane.

Drift – or, rather, Deadlock – led the way in his Earth car mode.

Once they were alone, Russell helped his dad to his feet and turned to Jetstorm with a nervous look on his face.

"So this is still all just an act, right? Drift hasn't betrayed us for real?" Russell asked anxiously.

"I guess we will soon find out," the mini-con replied.

CHAPTER NINE

"WHERE ARE WE HEADED, Deadlock?" Stilts asked, soaring through the air above the other three bots. "Maybe we can try out the old bomb-from-above move again – get it right this time!"

"No need," Drift replied. "The last Decepticon those do-gooders captured hid his stash in a car factory that should be deserted at this time of night. The native population does not understand Energon, so there was no risk of them stealing it for themselves."

Foxtrot banked to the right, nearly pushing Drift off the road.

"A deserted factory?" Foxtrot growled angrily. "I thought you were taking us somewhere we could cut loose and have some fun. If I'd just wanted to have a peaceful picnic, I'd have stayed in the woods."

Drift revved his motor and pulled ahead, kicking up dirt and rocks that bounced off Foxtrot's windscreen.

"There is no sense in exposing our existence to the humans until we are at full strength," Drift replied curtly.

He ground to a halt in front of an imposingly large factory, set far away from all the main roads and the houses and people of Crown City. The sun was down and all the factory workers had gone home.

The Ronin switched back into their bot modes, ready to rampage and nab some Energon.

"We'll scale the exterior and enter through the skylight," Drift said.

"No can do, old pal. This bot doesn't climb," Forager said, pointing to himself. "I ain't no good unless I got both my paws planted firmly on the ground. Why don't you stand back and let me take care of this."

The crafty crook popped a lockpick out of his claw to open the large delivery bay doors. Before he could finish tinkering with the lock, Foxtrot stepped forward, pulled out his blaster, and shot a hole through the door.

BLAM!

"Oops," he said sarcastically. "Trigger digit slipped."

"Get a load of this bot, will ya?" Forager said, slapping Foxtrot on the back. "That's why they call him the Trigger-Happy Terror!"

"That's not what I call him," Stilts replied with a smirk.

Foxtrot flashed his teeth at his comrade. "Quit grinding my gears," he snarled.

"Ah, shove it down your intake valve," Stilts retorted.

The bots piled inside, towering high in the building that was designed for people.

Stilts's cranium grazed the ceiling.

"Maybe I'd better wait outside," he said. "I'm not a big fan of tight spaces."

Foxtrot gave the bot a shove, telling him to keep moving and stop complaining.

Drift led the Ronin to a decommissioned part of the factory, blocked off with yellow caution tape. They smashed through equipment and knocked over car parts as they walked along.

"I see you have not mastered the art of stealth in my absence," Drift observed.

He directed them towards a hulking, tarp-covered shape and dramatically pulled the cover off.

The Decepticons had discovered a gargantuan, glowing stack of Energon cubes – ripe for the taking!

"Well, hello, beautiful!" Forager squeaked.

They each grabbed as many cubes as they could carry and turned to leave the way they had come in.

As they neared the exit, Drift was the first to spot a human security guard at the far end of a long hallway. The man was inspecting the smouldering remains of car parts that the Decepticons had trashed on their way in.

"This is Officer Wong," the man whispered into a walkie-talkie. "I need to report a serious break-in and a lot of damage."

Foxtrot's audio receptors perked up. He turned toward the sound and spied the human.

"Perfect," Foxtrot said, whipping out his blaster. "Some target practice!"

The Decepticon took aim, but Drift blocked his shot.

"You lack finesse, Foxtrot," Drift said. "I will handle this!"

In a flash, Drift unsheathed his sword and spun gracefully through the air. With a blur of movement, his blade sliced and diced the ceiling above them. Then he landed without even making a sound.

A moment later, a large portion of the hallway collapsed, leaving a pile of debris.

THUD!

"Wow! This samurai has got some style," Forager exclaimed. "These fleshbags don't stand a chance against that can opener of his!"

Foxtrot snarled with laughter and put away his blaster.

Meanwhile, on the other side of the rubble, a frightened but perfectly unharmed Officer Wong hightailed it to his police car and sped away.

With their stashed Energon in tow, the bots hustled out the exit and shifted into vehicle mode. Satisfied that their heist was complete, they blazed a trail back to the scrapyard.

Upon their return, the Decepticons dumped their loot near the captives. Their fluids were pumping from the caper, and they finally began to let down their guard around Drift.

As he reminisced about their old days together, Forager started re-enacting a particularly crazed fight. He waved his arms and fired his blaster all around.

"Then I tried to grease that gearhead's wheels, but he threatened to blow my gasket!" Forager said, finishing his story.

The crook laughed so hard he fell backwards. His exhaust pipe started to sputter and a noxious gas filled the air.

"Filth!" gasped Stilts, covering his beak. "That went right in my vents!"

Forager laughed even harder, and even Foxtrot managed to break a smile.

"Ah yes," said Drift, standing and drawing several shuriken from his waist. "I seem to remember bailing your bumper out using ... these!"

He slung the throwing stars across the scrapyard, right at the Autobots!

The sharp, spinning blades skidded through the bars of the cage, barely avoiding Denny, Russell and the two mini-cons, all of whom ducked and recoiled in fear.

The three Ronin laughed uproariously and continued telling old battle tales as they wandered off together through the scrapyard.

Once the Decepticons were out of sight, Russell noticed something tied to one of the stars.

It was a note that read:

Go now. Release the others.

Russell showed the note to his fellow captives, a slow smile dawning on each of their faces.

Drift was not a traitor after all!

Slipstream checked the bars near where the shuriken had entered and realised that his master had discreetly sliced through the cage door. The clever samurai had made a space large enough for everyone to climb out!

Quickly and quietly, the five escapees climbed out and slunk toward the command centre.

Upon reaching the control console, Fixit rapidly started typing, and within seconds the stasis pods containing Bumblebee, Strongarm, Sideswipe and Grimlock had all opened up.

WHOOSH!

Bumblebee popped up and shook the stasis freeze from his optics. Grimlock, Strongarm and Sideswipe did the same.

"Come on, team," Bumblebee said, standing up and rallying the bots. "It's time to catch that Drift!"

CHAPTER TEN

"BUMBLEBEE, NO!" RUSSELL
shouted as the Autobot leader shifted
into his vehicle mode. "It's not what you
think! Drift isn't a bad guy!"

"He could have fooled me," Bumblebee
responded. "He led us straight into an
ambush."

"That wasn't Drift," Russell explained.
"One of the Decepticons can make
holograms. Drift was a part of their gang
a long time ago, but he quit when they
were going to hurt a bunch of people.
Jetstorm and I helped Drift rejoin them
to rescue you!"

Bumblebee considered this information.

"It looks like I might owe Drift an apology if we make it out of this," Bumblebee said. "But right now we need to act before their scanners notice we're out of stasis. Let's go and help our team-mate, Autobots!"

Team Bee tore through the scrapyard and quickly came face to face with the Ronin outside the diner. Without pausing, they all leaped into battle!

Grimlock barrelled his massive bulk at Stilts, but the nimble bot immediately switched into his plane mode and flew out of reach. He fired at the Dinobot from up high. CHOOM!

Strongarm discharged her blaster at Forager, who scurried under a pile of old cars and tunnelled out of reach.

"You ain't putting me back in that cell, law-bot!" Forager screamed.

Sideswipe set his sights on Foxtrot, the most deceptive of the Ronin.

The young Autobot flipped through the air towards his target – only to smash right through a hologram instead! While Sideswipe regained his bearings, the real Foxtrot appeared and delivered a painful blow.

"Flashy but not too bright," the Decepticon said.

As the rest of the team fought the Decepticons, Bumblebee dashed straight towards Drift. The samurai warrior instinctively drew his sword.

"This is not as it appears, Bumblebee!" Drift shouted over the din.

"I am not a traitor."

Bumblebee ground to a halt right in front of the samurai-bot.

"I know, and I'm sorry for not trusting you earlier. Your past is behind you. But right now, we have a tough fight ahead of us, and we need to work together."

Bumblebee and Drift exchanged curt nods. As Bee joined Sideswipe's fight against Foxtrot, Drift caught up with Grimlock.

The frustrated Dinobot was hurling cars up at Stilts, with little success.

"Grimlock, catch!" Drift yelled to the Dinobot, tossing him a small object.

Grimlock looked down at the device. "This tiny thing?" he exclaimed. "I was having better luck with the cars."

"Trust me," Drift said.

The Dinobot stretched his arm back and threw the device at the flying Ronin.

"One lob-ball special, coming up!" he announced.

Upon impact, the capsule became an expanding net like the one Stilts had used to capture Slipstream and Denny.

The net tangled around the Decepticon's wings and brought him down in a crash landing.

SMASH!

"Let me out of here! I hate tight spaces!" Stilts cried, twisting and turning on the ground.

"Well you'd better get used to it," Grim told him. "Those stasis pods aren't exactly roomy!"

With Stilts dispatched, Drift and Grimlock sprinted over to find Strongarm struggling with Forager, who had tunnelled deep into a heap of junked cars. Every time Strongarm got close, Forager fired his blaster left and right, covering the area.

Drift scanned the area and saw the hydraulic lift machine.

"Strongarm, use that construction vehicle to remove his advantage!" Drift instructed her.

Strongarm, cautious about Drift's loyalty, leaped behind the wheel of the large lift.

Pulling one lever, Strongarm swung the machine around and knocked over most of the stacked cars, exposing Forager's hiding place. Then Strongarm flipped on the powerful magnetic field, which caught Forager and dragged the kicking and screaming Ronin high off the ground.

CLANG!

"Lemme go! Lemme go!" Forager yipped. "I don't like heights!"

"Hang in there," Strongarm said smugly.

She joined Drift and Grimlock, and the trio raced towards the fight against Foxtrot.

When they turned the corner, they found that Bumblebee and Sideswipe were not fighting the single Ronin – they were tussling with over fifty Foxtrots!

"Most of them are holograms, but the real Ronin keeps attacking us while we're distracted!" Sideswipe told Drift, bringing him up to speed.

Drift thought for a moment.

"Everybot stay calm and close your optics," Drift said.

"Are you trying to get us blasted?" Strongarm asked.

"Do what Drift says, cadet!" Bumblebee ordered. "Trust your instincts!"

The five Autobots stood totally silent, shoulder to shoulder and back to back. After a nanocycle of concentration, one noise broke through the din of holographic humming: the clinking of Foxtrot unlatching his sidearm!

"There!" the bots all shouted in unison.

Bumblebee, Strongarm and Sideswipe pointed their plasma cannons and fired.

The real Foxtrot took three simultaneous hits and staggered back.

Projection discs crunched underfoot as Grimlock trampled across the scrapyard, extinguishing holograms left and right.

Foxtrot tried to make a break for it, but Drift got a running start and tackled him to the ground.

"Ronin take care of their own," Drift said. "And you've been outfoxed."

He delivered a wallop of a punch right to Foxtrot's snout, knocking him out.

POW!

Grimlock brought one massive foot down on the Ronin's tail, preventing him from crawling away.

"You may have defeated the Ronin, Deadlock," Foxtrot whispered, as he struggled under Grimlock's weight. "But you can never change who you really are."

"There is no Deadlock, only Drift now," the reformed Autobot said.

"And Drift was never wicked like you to begin with," Bumblebee added.

The Autobot leader turned towards Drift and reached out his hand. "I apologise, Drift. I should have trusted you straight away."

"Your apology is not necessary, Bumblebee," Drift replied, shaking his hand. "I did not trust you all with my past, and it became a danger to us. It is not in my nature to be so ... open ... but I vow to do better."

The Autobots helped to carry the rest of the bad bots back to the stasis pods, where Russell, Denny and the mini-cons were waiting.

Drift bowed before Slipstream and Jetstorm.

"I humbly seek your forgiveness, students," he said.

Jetstorm and Slipstream looked at each other, unsure of how to respond. They bowed in return.

"We humbly grant it, master," the mini-cons replied in unison.

"Even though I am your master, I am still learning as well," Drift said quietly. "Today I have learned the virtue of trust, and that running from your past will only leave you to confront it alone and unprepared."

Grimlock surprised Drift with a big Dinobot embrace.

"Welcome back!" he cheered.

"It is also not in my nature ... to be so ... close," grunted Drift.

The Autobots all laughed and patted each other on the back, congratulating one another on another mission accomplished.

"I guess we *do* make a great team after all," Bumblebee said to Drift.

"And you make a great leader, Bumblebee," Drift replied. He bowed deeply to the yellow Autobot commander.

Bumblebee returned the gesture, bowing low in front of the samurai.

Then Drift helped his team-mates to load Foxtrot, Forager and Stilts into stasis pods. As the pods slid shut, locking away the Ronin criminals, Drift could feel his past as Deadlock finally disappearing with them.

He was no longer a Decepticon,
a masterless samurai or even a Ronin
fighting only for himself. He was an
Autobot, fighting for Earth … and for his
new friends!

· · · MISSION COMPLETE · · ·

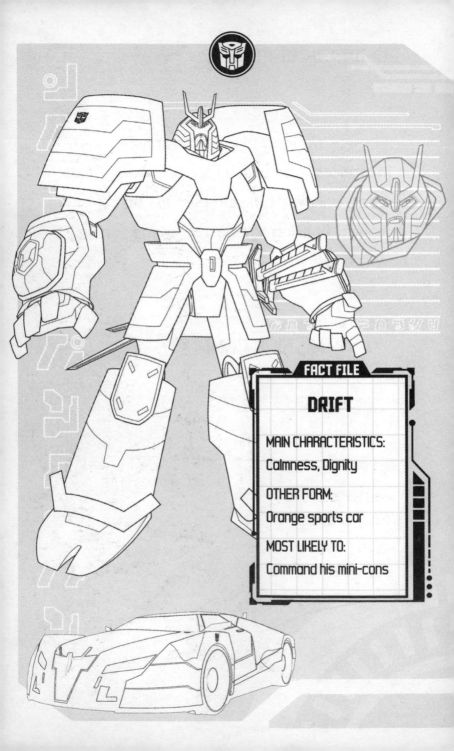

FACT FILE

DRIFT

MAIN CHARACTERISTICS:
Calmness, Dignity

OTHER FORM:
Orange sports car

MOST LIKELY TO:
Command his mini-cons

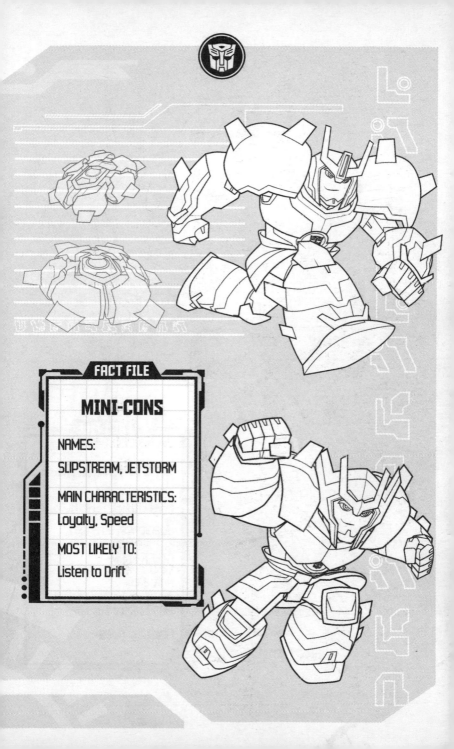

FACT FILE

MINI-CONS

NAMES:
SLIPSTREAM, JETSTORM

MAIN CHARACTERISTICS:
Loyalty, Speed

MOST LIKELY TO:
Listen to Drift

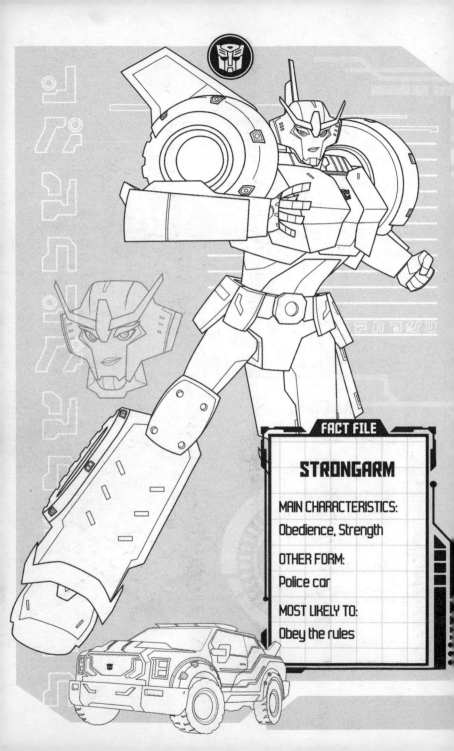

FACT FILE

STRONGARM

MAIN CHARACTERISTICS:
Obedience, Strength

OTHER FORM:
Police car

MOST LIKELY TO:
Obey the rules

FACT FILE

FIXIT

Fixit might not fight
Decepticons, but he's a
vital part of the team!

MAIN CHARACTERISTICS:
Engineering skill, Stutter

MOST LIKELY TO:
Fix things

THE ALL-NEW ACTION-PACKED ADVENTURES

OUT NOW ON DVD & DIGITAL HD

© 2016 Hasbro, all rights reserved.